Let's Fly from **A** to **Z**

Let's Fly from A to Z

Doug Magee and Robert Newman

COBBLEHILL BOOKS
Dutton   New York

To Ruth Magee, who taught me to keep my feet on the ground and my hopes in the clouds.

—D.M.

To the working mothers and fathers who have flown.

—R.N.

Library of Congress Cataloging-in-Publication Data

Magee, Doug, date
   Let's fly from A to Z / Doug Magee and Robert Newman.
      p.   cm.
   Summary: An alphabet book introducing the world of
   airplanes.
   ISBN 0-525-65105-5
   1. Airplanes—Juvenile literature. 2. English language—
   Alphabet—Juvenile literature. [1. Airplanes.
   2. Alphabet.] I. Newman, Robert. II. Title.
TL547.M25   1992
629.133′34—dc20
[E]   91-39774   CIP   AC

Published in the United States by Cobblehill Books, an
affiliate of Dutton Children's Books, a division of Penguin
Books USA Inc., 375 Hudson Street, New York, New York 10014

Designed by Charlotte Staub
Printed in Hong Kong
First Edition   10 9 8 7 6 5 4 3 2 1

Acknowledgments

We wish to thank the following for their help in the preparation
of this book: Dick Brouwer; Tony Bill; Sue T. Moss and the
people at United Airlines; Ron McComas, Lee Robins, and all
the others at Delta Airlines.

Let's fly from A to Z.
When do we take off? Right now!

A a

Airplanes fly in the sky. They take us from here to there by air.

There are big planes . . .

. . . and small planes.

An **airport** is where airplanes take off and land.
Passengers arrive by bus or car.

Bb

On an airplane, there is a lot of **baggage**. It goes in the **baggage compartment** under the plane.

Cc

A **controller** in the **control tower** tells the pilot when it is all right to take off or to land.

The plane's cabin has seats for the passengers.

Dd

The doors of a plane
fit tightly when closed.

An airplane's **elevators** are on the tail. The pilot moves them up or down to make the plane go up or down.

F f

The fuselage is the whole central body of the airplane.

Flaps on the wings give the plane more lift.
They are used on takeoff and landing.

Gg

The **galley** is where meals are prepared in flight.

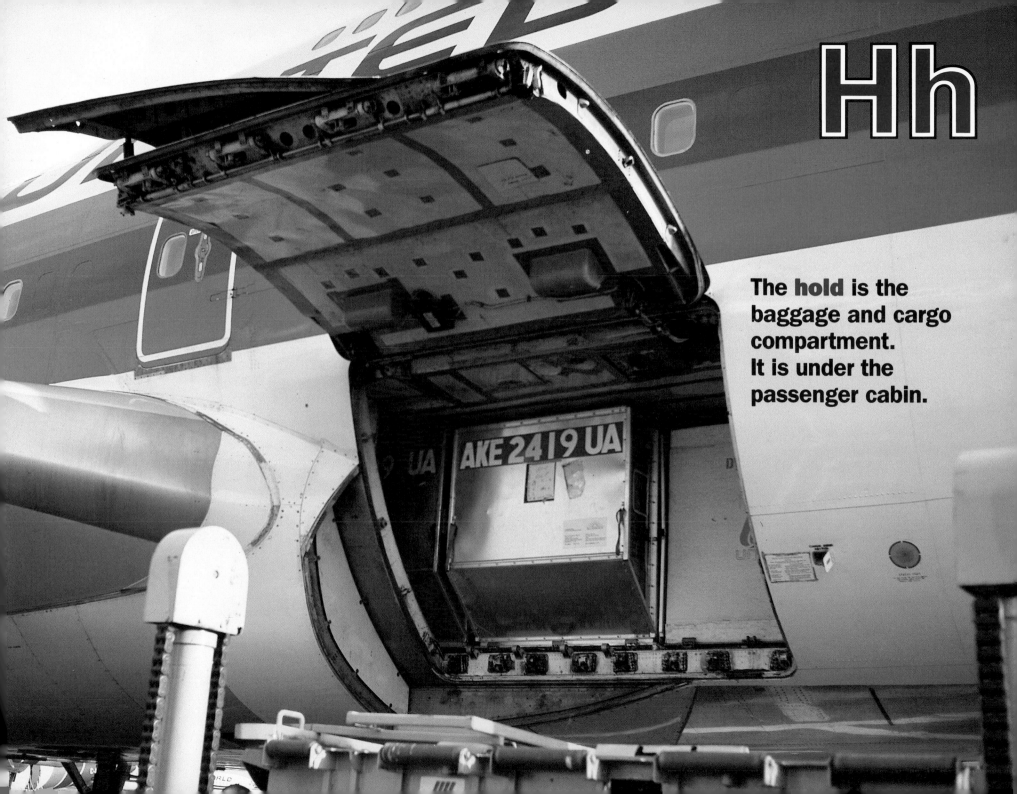

Hh

The **hold** is the baggage and cargo compartment. It is under the passenger cabin.

AKE 2419 UA

A **hangar** is a garage for airplanes. They can be repaired or stored there.

The instrument panel tells the pilot many things about the airplane—how high it is, where it is, how fast it is going.

Jj

A **jet engine** provides power for today's big planes. It thrusts the airplane forward.

Kk

Jet planes use **kerosene** as fuel.
It is pumped into tanks in the plane's wings.

The keel is the bottom of the fuselage.

On landing, the wheels touch down on the runway.

LI

Landing lights help the pilot
see the runway at night.

Navigation lights show which way the plane is headed—
red on the left, green on the right.

Mm

Mechanics inspect and maintain planes to keep them in good condition.

The **nose** is the front of the airplane.
It contains the cockpit where the pilot and co-pilot sit.

Oo

The opening
on a jet engine
looks like an o.

Some airplanes fly over the clouds.

Pp

Air rushing through **pitots** indicates the plane's speed on the instrument panel.

On some planes, a propeller thrusts the airplane forward.

The pilot talks to the control tower on the radio.

Q is **QUEBEC** in airplane radio talk. Special words are used instead of letters because they are easier to understand.

A ALPHA	I INDIA	O OSCAR	U UNIFORM
B BRAVO	J JULIET	P PAPA	V VICTOR
C CHARLEY	K KILO	Q QUEBEC	W WHISKEY
D DELTA	L LIMA	R ROMEO	X XRAY
E ECHO	M MIKE	S SIERRA	Y YANKEE
F FOXTROT	N NOVEMBER	T TANGO	Z ZULU
G GOLF			
H HOTEL			

Q q

Rr

The radio antenna lets the pilot and the control tower talk to one another.

The rudder on the tail fin turns the plane left . . . or right.

Ss

Seat belts **keep us safe.**

**A strut connects a
wheel to the airplane.**

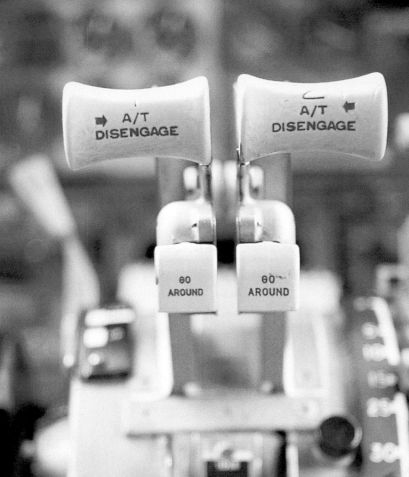

Tt

The throttle controls the speed of the engine.

Airplanes are towed away from the boarding gate.

Planes taxi to and from the runway under their own power.

On **takeoff**, the plane leaves the ground and climbs aloft.

Uu

The **undercarriage**—the wheels and landing gear—
is raised into the plane after takeoff,
and lowered for landing.

Vv

An outtake **valve** controls pressure in a plane.

A **vent** lets fumes and heat out of the engine.

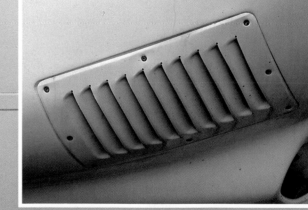

W w

Air flowing over and under the **wings** keeps the plane in the sky.

X is what some runways look like from the air.

X x

Yy

BEFORE TAKEOFF

FLAPS _____ _____

AFTER TAKEOFF

LANDING GEAR _____ OFF
FLAPS _____ UP

APPROACH

PRESSURIZATION _____ SET
AIRSPEED BUGS _____ SET
ALTIMETERS _____ SET
RECALL _____ CHECKED

LANDING

SPEEDBRAKE _____ ARMED
LANDING GEAR _____ DOWN
FLAPS _____

Using the yoke, the pilot controls the plane— up or down, left or right.

The altimeter tells the pilot how high the aircraft is. **Zero** indicates sea level.

Zz

An airplane zooms up into the sky.   Happy landing!

J629.
13334
MAG

Magee, Doug,
   1947-

Let's fly from A to
Z.

DATE		